BEAVERS BUILD LODGES

BY ELIZABETH RAUM   ILLUSTRATED BY ROMINA MARTÍ

AMICUS ILLUSTRATED and AMICUS INK are published by Amicus
P.O. Box 1329, Mankato, MN 56002
www.amicuspublishing.us

LIBRARY OF CONGRESS CATALOGING-IN-PUBLICATION DATA
Names: Raum, Elizabeth, author. | Martí, Romina, illustrator.
Title: Beavers build lodges / by Elizabeth Raum ; illustrated by Romina Martí.
Description: Mankato, Minnesota : Amicus Illustrated/Amicus Ink, [2018] |
    Series: Animal builders | Series: Amicus illustrated | Audience: K to grade 3. |
    Includes bibliographical references.
Identifiers: LCCN 2016048897| ISBN 9781681511689 (library binding) | ISBN
    9781681521497 (pbk.) | !ISBN 9781681512587 (e-book)
Subjects: LCSH: Beavers—Habitations—Juvenile literature. | Beavers—
    Behavior—Juvenile literature.
Classification: LCC QL737.R632 R38 2017 | DDC 599.371564—dc23
LC record available at https://lccn.loc.gov/2016048897

EDITOR: Rebecca Glaser
DESIGNER: Kathleen Petelinsek

Printed in the United States of America
HC 10 9 8 7 6 5 4 3 2 1
PB 10 9 8 7 6 5 4 3 2

ABOUT THE AUTHOR

As a child, Elizabeth Raum hiked through the Vermont woods searching for signs that animals lived nearby. She read every animal book in the school library. She now lives in North Dakota and writes books for young readers. Many of her books are about animals. To learn more, go to: www.elizabethraum.net.

ABOUT THE ILLUSTRATOR

Romina Martí is an illustrator who lives and works in Barcelona, Spain, where her ideas come to life for all audiences. She loves to discover and draw all kinds of creatures from around the planet, who then become the main characters for the majority of her work. To learn more, go to: rominamarti.com

It's spring! Beaver is off on a great adventure.
It's time to find a mate and build his own home.

Will the beaver find a mate? He leaves his scent on a pile of mud. It's a sign. A young female beaver sniffs the air.

Her nose leads her to the male. A perfect pair, they'll stay together for life.

A stream is nearby, but beavers need a pond. They'll have to build a dam. Beavers use their sharp front teeth to bite into trees. Then they gnaw the wood with their lower teeth. Timber! Trees crash to the ground.

Building a dam is hard work. The beavers float the logs on the water. They pile the logs across the stream. They weave branches together and add more logs.

In fast-moving water, beavers use rocks to hold the logs in place. They pack mud into the cracks. The dam is strong. It holds back the water. A pond takes shape.

Birds, fish, and other animals
move in to the beaver pond.
Some are friendly. Others are not.

A wolf! The beavers slap their tails on the water. CRACK! SPLASH! Animals and birds scatter. The beavers dive into the pond. They hide underwater for up to 15 minutes.

The wolf gave up. Now it's time to build a lodge. The safest place is the middle of the pond. Predators can't reach them there.

The beavers cut more trees
and pile the branches on
the bottom of the pond.
Soon, the pile is so tall it
pokes out of the water.
It forms a dome.

The lodge is almost done. The beavers cover it with mud, moss, and leaves. But there's no door. They swim underwater and dig two entrances.

They use their sharp claws to carve spaces inside the dome. The lodge has rooms for eating and for sleeping. The rooms stay warm. How cozy!

In fall, it's time to gather extra food. Beavers are herbivores. They eat wood and leafy plants. They drag leafy branches into the pond near the lodge. The deep, cold water will keep the food fresh all winter.

During winter, the beavers mate. Three months later, Mama Beaver gives birth to a litter of kits. Mama Beaver feeds the newborn kits milk and they grow quickly. Then their parents feed them leaves and twigs.

In summer, the beavers swim and play. They repair the dam and fix the lodge. The kits help. The parents teach them how to build and find food.

When the kits are two years old, they'll leave home to go on their own adventures and build their own lodges. Happy building, beavers!

Where Beavers Live

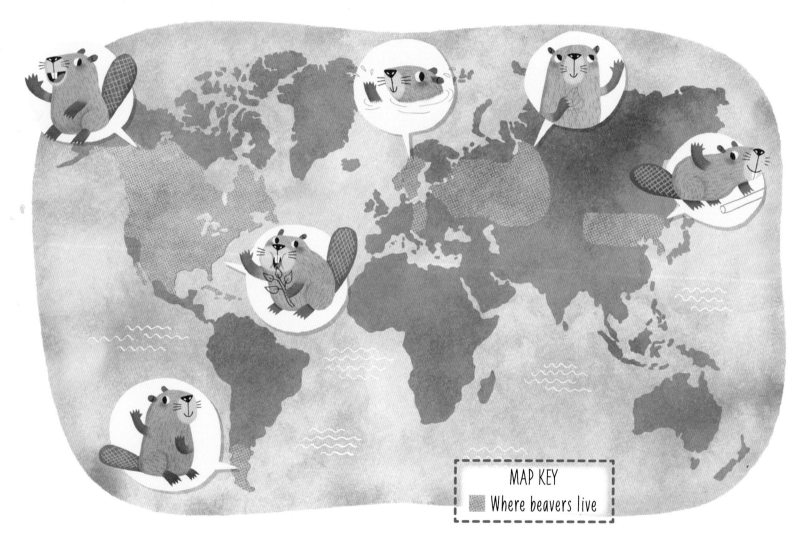

MAP KEY

Where beavers live

Build Like a Beaver

Beavers use items in their habitats to build dams and lodges.
Try building a model of a dam to see how they work.

WHAT BEAVERS USE	WHAT YOU NEED
Riverbed	9x13 inch (23x33 cm) disposable baking pan
	Play dough or clay
Logs and branches	Pop sticks
Mud	Play dough
Small stream	Pitcher of water

WHAT YOU DO

1. Cover the bottom of a baking pan with about 1 inch (2.5 cm) of play dough.

2. Carve a riverbed down the middle of the play dough.

3. Stack pop sticks across the riverbed to build a dam. Break the sticks into different lengths if you need to.

4. Use play dough to patch any gaps between the sticks.

5. Test your dam by gently pouring water into the river above the dam. Does it hold back the water? If not, try again.

GLOSSARY

dam A barrier built across a river or stream to stop the flow of water.

herbivore An animal that eats only plants.

kit A baby beaver.

lodge A beaver's home.

mate A partner; a pair who join together to breed young.

predator An animal that hunts other animals for food.

READ MORE

Gibbons, Gail. *Beavers*. New York: Holiday House, 2013.

Holland, Mary. *The Beavers' Busy Year*. Mt. Pleasant, South Carolina: Sylvan Dell Publishing, 2014.

Peterson, Megan Cooley. *Look Inside a Beaver's Lodge*. Mankato, Minn.: Capstone Press, 2012.

Riggs, Kate. *Beavers*. Mankato, Minn.: Creative Education, 2015.

WEBSITES

Animals: Beaver
http://kids.nationalgeographic.com/animals/beaver
Find photos and basic facts about beavers.

Beavers Are Geniuses
http://video.nationalgeographic.com/video/beaver_lifecycle
Watch beavers build a lodge.

Beaver Dams | Animal Planet
http://www.animalplanet.com/tv-shows/other/videos/fooled-by-nature-beaver-dams/
Watch beavers underwater as they store wood and then build a lodge.

Bob the Builder
https://www.nwf.org/Kids/Ranger-Rick/Animals/Mammals/Beavers.aspx
Read more about a beaver named Bob in this article from Ranger Rick.

Every effort has been made to ensure that these websites are appropriate for children. However, because of the nature of the Internet, it is impossible to guarantee that these sites will remain active indefinitely or that their contents will not be altered.